METAL LIKE ME

D.W. Saur

WITH ILLUSTRATION BY

DANIELLE GREEN

NEWMAN SPRINGS PUBLISHING
320 Broad Street
Red Bank, NJ 07701

First originally published by Newman Springs Publishing 2019

ISBN 978-1-64531-248-2 (Hardcover)
ISBN 978-1-64531-247-5 (Digital)

Printed in the United States of America

In memory of Kevin and Chris—

True friends who knew the meaning of pals

To my family and to the tunes that have provided more than just entertainment

D. W. Saur

To my little rock star, Crosley

Mommy

I WAS BORN INTO A FAMILY UNLIKE YOURS, WELL, PERHAPS LIKE YOURS.

I WAS BORN INTO A METAL MUSIC FAMILY, AND WE ARE WHAT PEOPLE CALL METALHEADS.

I WAS NAMED VINNY FREHLEY RHODES, AFTER THE DRUMMER VINNIE PAUL AND GUITARIST ACE FREHLEY, BOTH AMONG THE BEST IN THEIR FIELD.

METAL MUSIC IS LOUD, PLAYED FAST, AND ASSOCIATED WITH HEAD BANGING AND SCREAMING.

WHEN PEOPLE SEE HEAD BANGING AND HEAR THE SCREAMING, THEY THINK WE ARE UNHAPPY AND FULL OF ANGER.

THEY MAY BE SURPRISED TO KNOW THAT METALHEADS ARE SOME OF THE HAPPIEST PEOPLE ON EARTH.

IF THEY WERE *METAL LIKE ME*, THEY WOULD UNDERSTAND.

WHILE OTHERS GOT BEDTIME STORIES OF KNIGHTS, SUPERHEROES, OR OTHER BEINGS OF FANTASY, I GOT STORIES OF CONCERTS MY PARENTS WENT TO.

WHILE OTHERS LISTENED TO OLD MCDONALD, I LISTENED TO ALICE COOPER. WHILE OTHERS HAD PLAYDATES, I ATTEMPTED TO PLAY MY DAD'S OLD GUITAR WHILE WATCHING LIVE CONCERTS.

I NEVER NOTICED WE WERE DIFFERENT FROM OTHERS. I WAS ALWAYS SURROUNDED BY METALHEADS, SO I THOUGHT EVERYONE WAS *METAL LIKE ME.*

THINGS CHANGED AS I GOT OLDER. I NOTICED HOW PEOPLE TREATED US DIFFERENTLY FROM NON-METALHEADS.

SOME PEOPLE WANTED US TO BE SAD. THEY DID THINGS THAT WOULD MAKE MOST FEEL SELF-CONSCIOUS AND MISERABLE.

SOME OF THEM STARED AND WHISPERED TO EACH OTHER AS THEY SAW MY FAMILY WALKING BY IN OUR METAL T-SHIRTS, DYED HAIR, TATTOOED ARMS, AND MULTIPLE PIERCINGS.

IF THEY WERE *METAL LIKE ME*, THEY WOULD HAVE UNDERSTOOD.

SOMETIMES THEY SHOUTED, "*FREAK SHOW!*"

WHEN THEY DID, I IMMEDIATELY BROKE OUT SINGING AVATAR'S "*SMELLS LIKE A FREAK SHOW.*"

IF THEY WERE *METAL LIKE ME,* THEY WOULD HAVE UNDERSTOOD.

SOMETIMES THEY CALLED US, "GOTHS!"

WHEN THEY DID, I IMMEDIATELY STARTED SINGING "ALL HALLOWS EVE" BY MY FAVORITE GOTHIC BAND, TYPE O NEGATIVE.

IF THEY WERE METAL LIKE ME, THEY WOULD HAVE UNDERSTOOD.

IN ELEMENTARY SCHOOL I WAS AN OUTCAST. MY CRAFTS DISPLAYED BAND LOGOS, CONCERT SCENES, AND SELF-PORTRAITS OF ME AS A FRONT MAN. DURING SHOW-AND-TELL TIME, I WOULD PROUDLY DISPLAY MY NEW ALBUMS AND T-SHIRTS OR ATTEMPT TO PLAY A SONG. MY CLASSMATES DIDN'T TALK TO ME AND TEASED ME, BUT...

IF THEY WERE *METAL LIKE ME*, THEY WOULD HAVE UNDERSTOOD.

My lack of friends never kept me down, because I had my family and my metal to go home to.

However, things changed in middle school. I joined hundreds of new students in a much larger school.

I immediately thought I would find someone *METAL LIKE ME*.

For the first day of school, I wore a new Gama Bomb T-shirt, my cut-off jean jacket covered in band patches, and my favorite pair of jeans that were capped off by my favorite sneakers.

I walked into the gym and saw what seemed to be a couple thousand students sitting in the bleachers.

As I gazed around, I found an all-too-familiar sight. A student dressed all in black was sitting alone, isolated from the rest. You could fit twenty or thirty people in the empty space around him.

I could tell that he was *Metal Like Me*.

THE CLOSER I GOT TO THE STUDENT, THE MORE I COULD SEE HE WAS, IN FACT, A METALHEAD.

HIS ALL-BLACK ATTIRE, JET-BLACK HAIR COVERING MUCH OF HIS FACE, LEATHER WRIST GAUNTLETS, AND WHAT APPEARED TO BE AN AMON SHIRT TOLD ME THAT HE WAS INTO HEAVY METAL AND, POSSIBLY, EVEN DARK METAL.

UPON TAKING A SEAT, HE IMMEDIATELY SAID, "NICE SHIRT."

"YOU TOO. I'M VINNY."

"JASON," HE SAID.

AND WE SAT THERE IN SILENCE—THAT IS, UNTIL WE WERE JOINED BY A THIRD.

SHE WAS PALE WHITE, HAD BLACK FISHNET STOCKINGS AND ARM WARMERS, WITH BOOTS UP TO HER KNEES. HER LIPS, EYES, AND NAILS WERE PAINTED BLACK. CLEARLY, SHE WAS INTO GOTHIC AND DOOM METAL.

"LISA," SHE SAID AS SHE TOOK A SEAT.

"VINNY."

"JASON."

IT WAS AN AWKWARD, BUT YET COMFORTING, SILENCE. THREE PEOPLE WHO WEREN'T USED TO MAKING FRIENDS AND WHO WEREN'T USED TO CARRYING ON A CONVERSATION WITH ANOTHER STUDENT TOOK COMFORT IN KNOWING THEY WEREN'T ALONE.

T WASN'T LONG BEFORE THE THREE BECAME FIVE. CHRISTOPHER WAS OUR FOLK METAL REPRESENTATIVE. HE WORE A KILT WITH A KORPIKLANNI SHIRT, HAD DREADS, AND WAS WEARING COMBAT BOOTS THAT WERE SIMILAR TO JASON'S.

LASTLY, TAKA TOOK A SEAT NEXT TO LISA. BOTH WERE DRESSED SIMILARLY, BUT TAKA HAD A MORE THEATRICAL LOOK AS THOUGH SHE BELONGED ONSTAGE WITH A SYMPHONY BACKING HER VOCALS. SHE LOVED SYMPHONIC METAL.

MY NEW FRIENDS WERE *METAL LIKE ME.*

IDDLE SCHOOL IS THE PLACE WHERE PEOPLE FORM CLICKS. IT'S WHERE CHILDHOOD FRIENDS TEND TO PART TO MAKE NEW FRIENDS. BUT FOR THOSE *METAL LIKE ME*, IT CAN BE TOUGH.

AS THE MONTHS PASSED, MY GROUP FOUND STRENGTH IN NUMBERS. NOTHING AND NO ONE BOTHERED US WHEN WE WERE TOGETHER. OUR CONFIDENCE SOARED TO NEW LEVELS, AND PEOPLE LEFT THE GROUP ALONE.

IT WAS A DIFFERENT STORY WHEN WE WERE APART. WE WERE ALL PICKED ON OR BULLIED IN SOME WAY—HARSH WORDS, A PUSH INTO THE LOCKERS, OR SOMEONE WOULD SLAP BOOKS OUT OF OUR HANDS. THESE WERE THE MOST COMMON ASSAULTS.

S INDIVIDUALS, WE NEVER STOOD UP FOR OURSELVES. WE THOUGHT WE WOULD GET INTO MORE TROUBLE, SO WE DID WHAT ANY OTHER MIDDLE SCHOOL STUDENT WOULD DO.

WE BOTTLED IT UP, AND SOMETIMES TEACHERS WOULD NOTICE WHEN WE WERE GENUINELY SAD OR ANGRY. THEY THOUGHT IT WAS BECAUSE OF BEING METAL, SO THEY WOULD SAY, "DON'T WORRY, IT'S JUST A PHASE. YOU'LL GROW OUT OF IT."

IF ONLY THEY WERE *METAL LIKE ME*, THEY WOULD HAVE UNDERSTOOD.

JUST WANTED PEOPLE TO UNDERSTAND THAT TO ME, METAL WASN'T A PHASE, ABOUT A MESSAGE, OR ANYTHING ELSE.

TO ME, METAL IS ABOUT BEING FREE. I GET LOST IN THE MUSIC, AS IF I AM ALONE IN A FIELD WHERE MY CARES ARE GONE AND THE SOUNDS HIT MY EARS LIKE WAVES CRASHING ONTO A BEACH.

IT'S ABOUT A FEELING. THERE IS ALWAYS A SONG THAT CAN MATCH MY MOOD AND INSTANTLY MAKE ME FEEL BETTER, EVEN IF I'M HAPPY. THAT'S RIGHT, METAL CAN MAKE ME HAPPIER THAN HAPPY.

IT WAS NOW THE END OF SIXTH GRADE, AND I HAD A MISSION. I WAS GOING TO SHOW MY PEERS AND MY TEACHERS ANOTHER SIDE OF METAL.

IT WAS GOING TO BE A SIDE THAT GOES BEYOND A SHIRT, TORN JEANS, LONG HAIR, AND AWESOME MUSIC.

THIS SIDE LIVED OUTSIDE THE SHADOWS OF THE CLASSROOM, HALLWAYS, GYM, OR CAFETERIA.

THEN SUDDENLY IT HIT ME, A PLAN. I KNEW HOW TO GET PEOPLE TO LOOK AT US IN A DIFFERENT LIGHT AND FOR THEM TO SEE METAL IN ANOTHER WAY.

I MET WITH THE GROUP AND REVEALED MY IDEA. WE WERE NO LONGER GOING TO BE SILENT IN CLASS. INSTEAD, WE WERE GOING TO ANSWER EVERY QUESTION POSSIBLE. IN ADDITION, WE WERE GOING TO HELP OUR PEERS BY STARTING A PEER TUTORING CLUB. EACH ONE OF US WILL USE OUR ACADEMIC STRENGTHS TO HELP OTHERS.

I EVEN HAD A PLAN FOR OUTSIDE OF THE CLASSROOM. SINCE WE WERE FAIRLY ATHLETIC, WE WERE GOING TO TRY OUT FOR SPORTS. THIS WOULD HELP OTHERS SEE THE MORE SOCIAL SIDE OF US.

L ASTLY, WE WERE GOING TO DO SOMETHING FOR US. WE WERE GOING TO FORM A BAND TO DISPLAY OUR PASSION FOR THE THING THAT HAD DEFINED US.

THE METALHEADS WERE GOING TO SHOW THAT THERE'S MORE TO US THAN MEETS THE EYE.

THE START OF THE NEW SCHOOL YEAR BROUGHT OUT A NEW STUDENT IN EACH ONE OF US.

OUR PARTICIPATION CONFUSED OUR FELLOW CLASSMATES, AND OUR SUCCESS IN ATHLETICS BROUGHT ABOUT A CHANGE IN ATTITUDE TOWARD THE GROUP.

We were no longer the outcasts or misfits. The bullying decreased so much that by Christmas break we couldn't remember the last time something bad happened to us.

There was only one thing that wasn't going well and that was PT (Peer Tutoring).

For months the tutoring sessions only had a handful of visitors, but that all changed one day in March.

About fifteen minutes into the session, the library door slowly opened. In came over a dozen students.

All were quiet until Becca asked, "Is this peer tutoring?"

Taka popped up and answered, "You found it!"

OR THE NEXT FORTY-FIVE MINUTES THE METALHEADS HELPED OUR PEERS IN ALL THE CORE SUBJECTS AND SOME ELECTIVES.

A T THE END OF TUTORING WE WERE APPROACHED BY BECCA, THE EIGHTH GRADE CLASS PRESIDENT.

"I HEAR YOU GUYS HAVE A BAND."

"WE DO," LISA REPLIED.

"THE STUDENT COUNCIL WAS WONDERING IF YOU WOULD PLAY AT THE EIGHTH GRADE DANCE."

ALL OF US WERE IN SHOCK, AND NO ONE ANSWERED UNTIL LISA ASKED, "REALLY? US?"

"YOU DO KNOW THAT WE AREN'T THE POP SCHOOL BAND, RIGHT?" JUSTIN ASKED.

"WE DO. WE JUST ASK THAT YOU DON'T COVER ANYTHING TOO HEAVY," SHE SAID AS SHE WALKED OUT THE LIBRARY.

WE WENT ON TO NOT ONLY PLAY THE EIGHTH GRADE DANCE, BUT ALL THE SCHOOL DANCES UNTIL WE GRADUATED.

THE GROUP CONTINUED TO PLAY SPORTS AND TUTOR OUR PEERS. UPON GRADUATING, I WAS CERTAIN WE LEFT OUR MARK AND PERHAPS CHANGED PEOPLE'S OPINION OF METALHEADS.

ND SO IT ENDS, THE STORY OF HOW FIVE METALHEADS WENT FROM INFAMOUS TO BEING ACCEPTED.

IT TOOK ME AWHILE TO REALIZE THAT PEOPLE DON'T NEED TO BE METAL LIKE ME.

THEY JUST NEED TO KNOW THAT I AM METAL AND SO MUCH MORE.

About the Author and Illustrator

The dynamic duo of Saur-Green began with D. W.'s concept of the *Like Me* series in 2016, but the two had met almost a decade prior to their partnership while students at Roanoke College. While in a group work activity, Danielle's *Tool* T-shirt sparked a music conversation that has been ongoing ever since. Due to her incredible artwork, D. W. knew she was an excellent choice for the series, and thankfully, she was happy to join the team.

Professionally, Danielle is an art teacher for K-5 students and D. W. is a middle school history teacher. Danielle has always had a dream to become an illustrator, but D. W.'s goal of writing professionally is relatively new. It is difficult for the duo to say what the future holds, but it is certain that *Metal Like Me* is the catalyst to a new adventure.

Follow and Visit for Updates
@D.W.SAUR
@ARTWITHMRSGREEN
HTTPS://SAUR-GREENBOOKS.WEEBLY.COM/